MW00914231

CHRISTMAS PLANNER AND ORGANIZER

Museum of Fine Arts, Boston

RIZZOLI
NEW YORK

First published in the
United States of America in 1991 by
RIZZOLI INTERNATIONAL PUBLICATIONS, INC.
300 Park Avenue South
New York, NY 10010 and
Museum of Fine Arts, Boston
465 Huntington Avenue
Boston, MA 02115

Designed by Christina Bliss

ISBN 0-8478-1409-2

91 92 93 94 95 / 10 9 8 7 6 5 4 3 2 1

Printed and bound in Hong Kong

CONTENTS

Hark!
the herald
angels sing . . .

CHRISTMAS CARDS

Name	Sent	Received	Name	Sent	Received
Bartos					
Rolf, M + Mrs					
Roman					
Katie + Woodie					
Bunting, M + Mrs					
Bunting, Jan					

CHRISTMAS CARDS

Name	Sent	Received	Name	Sent	Received

CHRISTMAS CARDS

Name	Sent	Received	Name	Sent	Received

CHRISTMAS CARDS

Name	Sent	Received	Name	Sent	Received

Christ
the Savior
is born!

CHRISTMAS CARDS

Name	Sent	Received	Name	Sent	Received

CHRISTMAS CARDS

Name	Sent	Received	Name	Sent	Received

CHRISTMAS CARDS

Name	Sent	Received	Name	Sent	Received

*O hear
the angel
voices!*

CHRISTMAS CARDS

Name	Sent	Received	Name	Sent	Received

CHRISTMAS CARDS

Name	Sent	Received	Name	Sent	Received

Peace
on earth
and
mercy
mild . . .

CHRISTMAS CARDS

Name	Sent	Received	Name	Sent	Received

CHRISTMAS CARDS

Name	Sent	Received	Name	Sent	Received

CHRISTMAS CARDS

Name	Sent	Received	Name	Sent	Received

CHRISTMAS CARDS

Name	Sent	Received	Name	Sent	Received

Radiant

beams

from

Thy holy

face . . .

CHRISTMAS CARDS

Name	Sent	Received	Name	Sent	Received

CHRISTMAS CARDS

Name	Sent	Received	Name	Sent	Received

CHRISTMAS CARDS

Name	Sent	Received	Name	Sent	Received

Angels
from the
realms of
glory...

CHRISTMAS CARDS

Name	Sent	Received	Name	Sent	Received

CHRISTMAS CARDS

Name	Sent	Received	Name	Sent	Received

Bearing

gifts

we traverse

so far. . .

PRESENTS

FAMILY

Name / Item

Date

PRESENTS

FAMILY

Name / Item

Date

PRESENTS

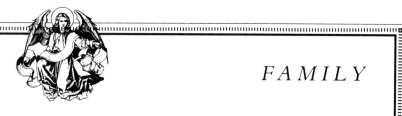

FAMILY

Name / Item   *Date*

PRESENTS

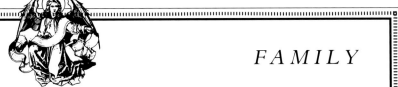

FAMILY

Name / Item   *Date*

Repeat

the

sounding

joy...

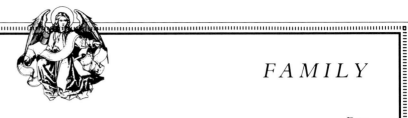

PRESENTS

FAMILY

Name / Item   *Date*

PRESENTS

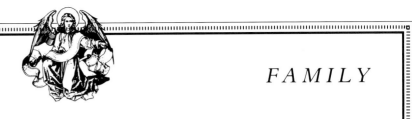

FAMILY

Name / Item   *Date*

Name / Item   *Date*

Glories

stream

from

heaven afar. . .

PRESENTS

FAMILY

Name / Item   Date

PRESENTS

FAMILY

Name / Item   *Date*

Heav'nly
hosts
sing
Alleluia . . .

PRESENTS

FRIENDS

Name / Item

Date

PRESENTS

FRIENDS

Name / Item

Date

PRESENTS

FRIENDS

Name / Item

Date

PRESENTS

FRIENDS

Name / Item

Date

Venite

Adoremus,

Dominum . . .

PRESENTS

FRIENDS

Name / Item

Date

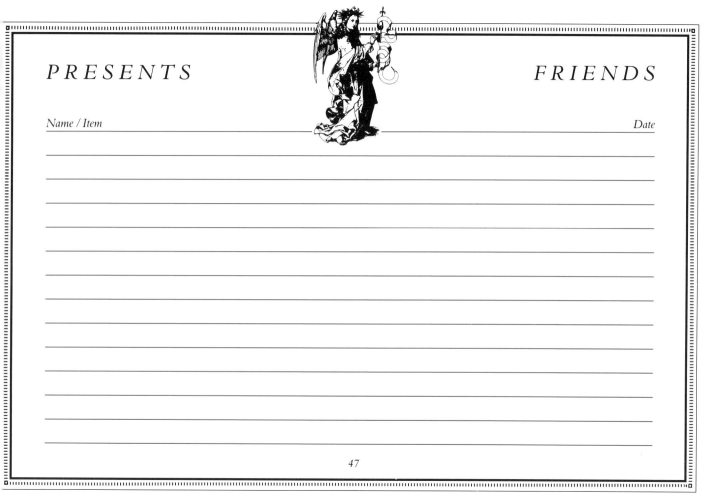

PRESENTS

FRIENDS

Name / Item

Date

Angels
we have
heard
on high . . .

PRESENTS

BUSINESS

Name / Item   *Date*

PRESENTS

BUSINESS

Name / Item   *Date*

PRESENTS

BUSINESS

Name / Item

Date

Glory to the newborn King...

HOLIDAY ENTERTAINING

Guest

Menu

HOLIDAY ENTERTAINING

Guest

Menu

HOLIDAY ENTERTAINING

Guest

Menu

HOLIDAY ENTERTAINING

Guest

Menu

Gloria
in excelsis
Deo...

HOLIDAY ENTERTAINING

Guest

_____

_____

_____

_____

_____

_____

_____

_____

_____

_____

_____

Menu

_____

_____

_____

_____

_____

_____

_____

_____

_____

_____

_____

HOLIDAY ENTERTAINING

Guest

Menu

INDEX

PAGE 45
Neri di Bicci
Italian (Florentine), 1419–about 1491
Virgin and Child Enthroned with Angels
Tempera on panel, 60⅞ × 35 in.
Charles Potter Kling Fund
1983.300

PAGE 48
Pieter de Witte (called Pietro Candido)
Flemish (worked in Florence and Munich),
about 1548–1628
The Mystical Marriage of St. Catherine (detail)
Oil on canvas, 89 × 62⅝ in.
Henry H. and Zoë Oliver Sherman Fund
1980.72

PAGE 49
Angel detail adapted from:
Marcantonio Raimondi
Italian, about 1480–about 1530
The Martydom of St. Félicité
Engraving after Raphael
Gift of Mrs. Lydia Evans Tunnard, in memory of
W.G. Russell Allen
64.2234

PAGE 52
From the **Book of Hours**
French, 15th century
"Adoration of the Magi" (detail) .
Gold and tempera on vellum with leather binding
18.5 × 14.0 × 4.0 cm.
The Gardner Brewer Collection
Bequest of Mrs. Arthur Croft
01.6751

PAGE 57
Gherardo Starnina
Italian (Florentine), 1354–1409/13
Jeremiah with Two Angels (detail)
Tempera on panel
Gift of Mrs. Thomas O. Richardson
20.1857

NOTES

NOTES